Tracey Wille

ROOSTER WRANGLING

Julia Krasnitski

Dedicated to Zac

We bought some eggs to grow ten hens.
We kept them until they hatched and then
We loved and raised our baby peeps,
And listened to their sweet, neat cheeps.

Soon they grew to run and play
And hang out in the yard all day.
Early when our chicks would wake,
We'd check for eggs they soon
should make.

But then one morning...

1 COCK a DOODLE DOO

One chicken was
a rooster dude!
Mom said **"No!"** and
Dad said **"Go!"**

We couldn't keep them if they crowed.
So we wrangled Rooster Number One;
And shipped him off to Washington.

Then the next morning...

2

COCK-A-DOODLE-DEEDLE-DOO!

Into the yard my parents flew!

Mom's wide eyes showed
GREAT SURPRISE;
Another rooster in disguise.

So we wrangled Rooster Number Two;

Now he's climbing mountains in Peru.

The morning after in dawn's light,
Everything appeared all right.
Until suddenly...

COCK-A-DOODLE-DOODLE-DEE!

How many roosters could there be?

So we wrangled Rooster Number Three;

He's taking the train to Italy.

4

When I listened in on morning four
I knew another was next door.
COCK-A-DOODLE-DOO-WOP-BOP!
Our egg-selling business
would be a flop.

So we wrangled Rooster Number Four;
He's on his way to Singapore.

5

Morning five was just the same;

One more chick was not a dame.

COCK-A-DOODLE-HOODLE-OO!

Our chances for eggs were getting few.

So we wrangled Rooster Number Five,
And in Japan he'll soon arrive.

I hoped and prayed on morning six

To hear no crows from our four chicks.

But... **COCK-A-DOODLE-DOODLEY-DOO!**

By then I knew just what to do.

So we wrangled Rooster Number Six
And sent him to Australia- Quick!

7

On day seven as rain fell down
I checked for eggs all around.
But then again to my dismay,

COCK-A-DOODLE-OODLE-AY!

So we wrangled Rooster Number Seven;

His plane to Kenya leaves at eleven.

8

I waited around on morning eight
To find out the next chick's fate.
COCK-A-DOODLE-NOODLE-DOO!
We wouldn't be naming that one Sue.

So we wrangled Rooster Number Eight;

He's exploring sand dunes in Kuwait.

9

Morning number nine was fine;

Two chicks were soaking up sunshine.

But before we made it to the coop—

COCK-A-DOODLE-OODLE-OOP!

So we wrangled Rooster Number Nine;

He'll find Egypt just divine.

10

One chick left on morning ten.
Could it, would it, be a hen?
Our wish was not to be for long.

COCK a DOOdle
DOOdle
DONG

So we wrangled Rooster Number Ten;
He's gone to England
to see Big Ben.

Now all our chicks have gone away,
But Mom brought home **NEW EGGS TODAY!**

About the Author

Tracey Willet resides in rural Maryland with her family and a small flock of egg-laying hens. She dreams about traveling to all of the places her fictional roosters get to go.

About the Illustrator

A Maryland artist, Julia Krasnitski remembers collecting eggs on her grandparents' farm as a child. Nowadays, however, she limits her interaction with wildlife to drawing playful animals and chasing her 4-year-old around the yard. You can visit her at juliakrasnitski.com.

About Atmosphere Press

Atmosphere Press is an independent, full-service publisher for excellent books in all genres and for all audiences. Learn more about what we do at atmospherepress.com.

We encourage you to check out some of Atmosphere's latest releases, which are available at Amazon.com and via order from your local bookstore:

Gloppy, by Janice Laakko
Wildly Perfect, by Brooke McMahan
How Grizzly Found Gratitude, by Dennis Mathew
Do Lions Cry?, by Erina White
Sadie and Charley Finding Their Way, by Bonnie Griesemer
Silly Sam and the Invisible Jinni, by Shayla Emran Bajalia
Feeling My Feelings, by Shilpi Mahajan
Zombie Mombie Saves the Day, by Kelly Lucero
The Fable King, by Sarah Philpot
Blue Goggles for Lizzy, by Amanda Cumbey
Neville and the Adventure to Cricket Creek, by Juliana Houston
Peculiar Pets: A Collection of Exotic and Quixotic Animal Poems, by Kerry Cramer
Carlito the Bat Learns to Trick-or-Treat, by Michele Lizet Flores
Zoo Dance Party, by Joshua Mutters
Beau Wants to Know, a picture book by Brian Sullivan
The King's Drapes, a picture book by Jocelyn Tambascio
You are the Moon, a picture book by Shana Rachel Diot
Onionhead, a picture book by Gary Ziskovsky
Odo and the Stranger, a picture book by Mark Johnson
Jack and the Lean Stalk, a picture book by Raven Howell

CPSIA information can be obtained
at www.ICGtesting.com
Printed in the USA
BVHW020926110122
625980BV00016B/337

9 781639 881147